SLOW LORIS

Alexis Deacon

SLOW LORIS

*'Deacon is undoubtedly a
welcome new talent'*

*'Alexis Deacon has tremendous
strengths as an artist and designer'*

*'The great pleasure of this book is
the quality of the illustrations'*

'Unusual and excellent'

*'This book, like Loris, is the
coolest thing around'*

*'Deacon's deadpan humour and
wonderfully expressive illustrations
in a sombre palette demand
constant re-readings'*

'A stunning picture book debut'

SLOW LORIS

LORIS

Alexis Deacon

RED FOX

For Tokyo (a tortoise)
and Rebecca (a girl)

SLOW LORIS
A RED FOX BOOK 978 0 099 41426 1

First published in Great Britain by Hutchinson,
an imprint of Random House Children's Publishers UK

Hutchinson edition published 2002
Red Fox edition published 2003

10

Red Fox Books are published by Random House Children's Publishers UK,
61-63 Uxbridge Road, London W5 5SA,
a division of The Random House Group Ltd,
Addresses for companies within The Random House
Group Limited can be found
at: www.randomhouse.co.uk/offices.htm

THE RANDOM HOUSE GROUP Limited Reg. No. 954009
www.randomhousechildrens.co.uk

A CIP catalogue record for this book is available from the British Library.

Printed in Malaysia

Slow Loris lived in a zoo
though he didn't care for it much.

Slow Loris wasn't his real name but that was what everyone called him.

A slow loris is just a type of animal.

Slow Loris was a slow loris.

He really was ...

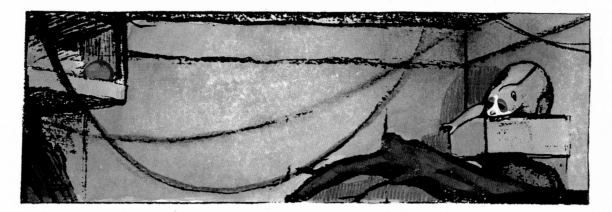

very ...

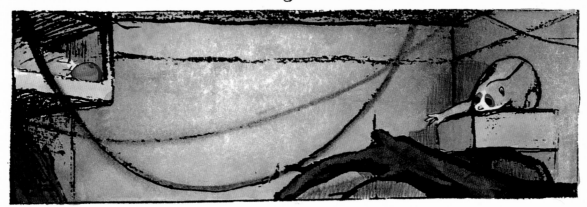

slow.

It took Loris ten minutes
to eat a satsuma...

twenty minutes to get from one

end of his

branch

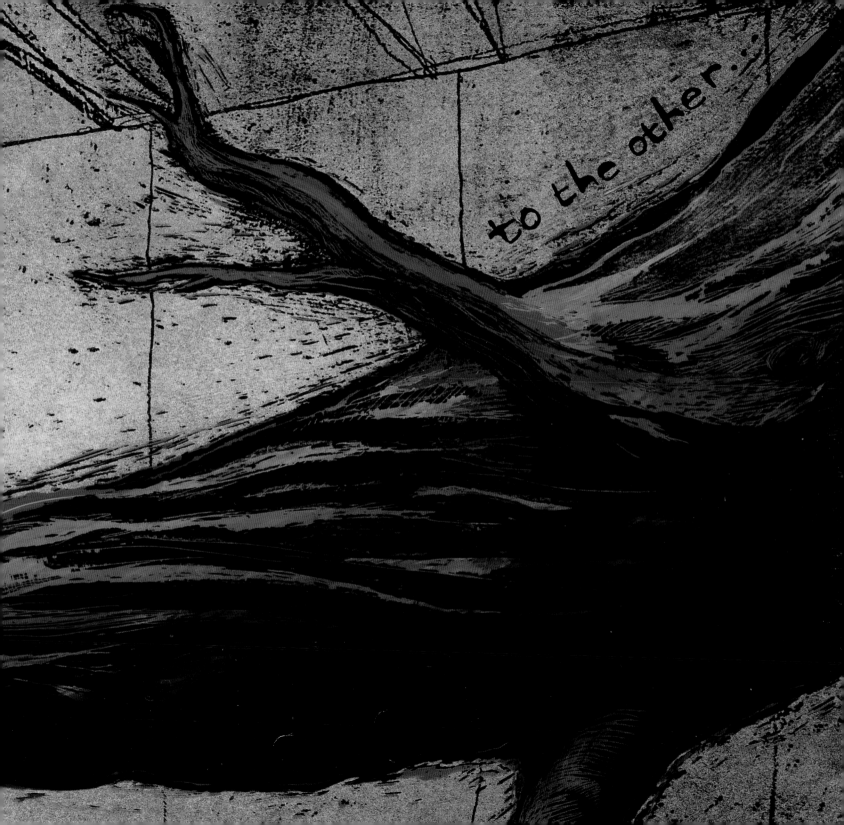

to the other.

and an hour to scratch his bottom.

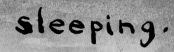

Most of the time though

he just hung around

sleeping.

The visitors all thought Loris was boring.

The other animals thought so too.

But he didn't care.

Loris had a secret.

At night, when all the other animals were sound asleep,

Loris got up

and did things...

FAST...

One night when Loris was busy

doing particularly noisy things...

News of Loris's secret life spread quickly.

Next evening the whole zoo gathered
outside the slow loris cage.

Sure enough, when it was really dark...

out

came

Loris.

The other animals were amazed. Loris wasn't boring at all. He was really wild.

That night they all did things together...

until they were

all so tired, not

one of them

could do another

thing.

The next day all the animals were slow. 'Boring!' said the visitors. But, like Loris, they didn't care, now they had a secret too.